HiLDeGARDe

and the

GREAT
GREEN
SHIRT
FACTORY

Written and Illustrated by
Ravay Snow

Snowbound Press

For Jon

With special thanks to Mom, Dad and Jeff

Snowbound Press
P.O. Box 698
Littleton, CO 80160-0698
www.snowboundpress.com

The artwork was executed in watercolor, gouache, pencil,
and colored inks on Arches cold press paper.
The text was set in Joulliard.

Book design by Kay Turnbaugh

No sheep, actual or fictional, were harmed during the course of this story.

Hildegarde™ is a vegetarian and uses all vegetable-based dyes in her designs.

Printed in Korea
First edition, Winter 2003

Second Printing

Publisher's Cataloging-in-Publication
(Provided by Quality Books, Inc.)

Snow, Ravay.
Hildegarde and the great green shirt factory / Ravay Snow.-1st ed.
p. cm.
SUMMARY : Hildegarde, an artistic sheep, expresses her creative side at work,
with unexpected results.
Audience: Ages 3-7.
LCCN 2003091242
ISBN 1-932362-10-X

1. Sheep-Juvenile fiction. 2. Creative ability-Juvenile fiction.
[1. Sheep-Fiction. 2. Creative ability-Fiction.] I. Title.

PZ7.S685128Hi 2003 [E] QBI33-1222

Every day, Hildegarde sewed 500 identical arms onto 250 identical shirts at the Great Green Shirt Factory. Great Green Shirts didn't seem so great to her. They should be called Ordinary Green Shirts, she felt.

"Boring!" thought Hildegarde.

She liked new experiences. She loved variety. And . . .

. . . she preferred unusual things.

On the walk to work
that morning,

she had found

a ball of
pink tinfoil,

five sparkly
sequins,

and a length
of tinsel.

Hildegarde used them
to make her own Great Green shirt
different from everyone else's.

She loved it.
So did the rest of the ewes
who worked with her in the
sewing room – all 139 of them!
Everyone clapped as Hildegarde
and her friend, Toola, danced.

The tinsel swished like a ballgown.

**What fun
they were having!**

Until
Mr. Arno
stomped in.

Mr. Arno
didn't like
his workers
to have fun.

He liked things
to be predictable.

He loved routine.

And he hated anything
that was out of the ordinary.

"What is going on here?"

In a meek voice, Hildegarde asked,
"How do you like my shirt design?"

Mr. Arno's nostrils flared angrily.

Hildegarde stammered, "I – I – I think that making shirts
in different styles would be good! Maybe even in different
colors! Sheep would like variety!"

Mr. Arno's eyes bulged. His ears quivered.

Hildegarde steeled herself to be shouted at,
but Mr. Arno did something worse.

He tore the foil from her shirt and tossed it away.
The tinsel and sequins followed…

until Hildegarde's
shirt was the same as
everyone else's.

"Why do you think you could design anything better than a Great Green Shirt?" Mr. Arno's voice echoed through the room.

"You're just a ewe!"

He stormed away.

One tear trickled from Hildegarde's eye.

She slunk back to her sewing machine and sewed identical sleeves onto identical shirts all afternoon.

That night, she couldn't sleep.

Whenever she closed her eyes,
she heard Mr. Arno's words.
Maybe he was right.
After all, she was just a ewe.

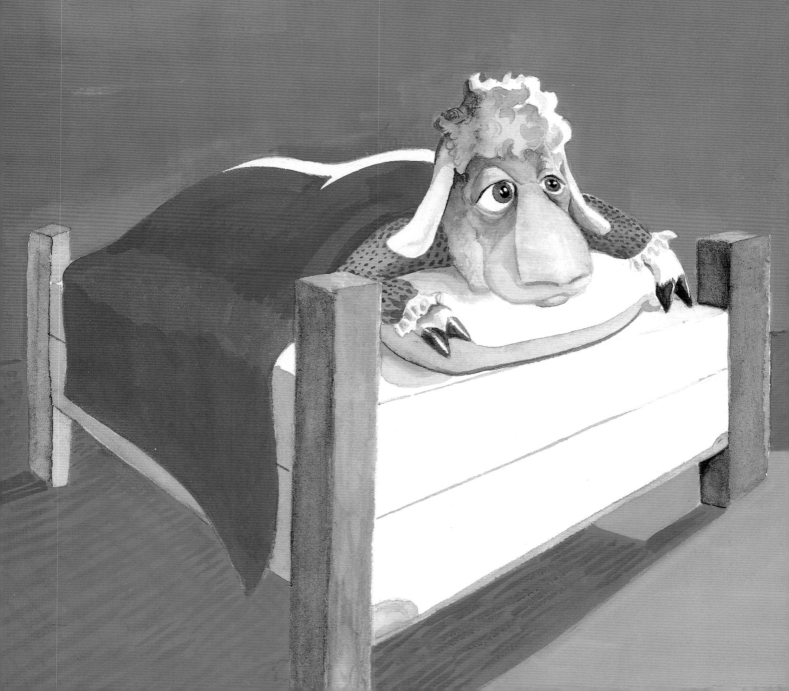

She couldn't sleep the next night either.

Or the night after that.

Hildegarde tried counting sheep. But they always turned out to be friends of hers.

She would get into conversations with them that left her wider-awake than ever.

She tried other things.

She fixed

midnight snacks.

And 2 o'clock snacks.

And 4 o'clock snacks.

She read boring books.

But she still couldn't sleep.
When she started to drift off,
she would hear Mr. Arno's words
and feel wide-awake again.

One night, Hildegarde learned to knit. By sunrise, she finished a sweater. But seeing it in the dawn light, she could tell something was missing. She concentrated. Then she picked up a beautiful fuchsia ribbon and wove it into the sweater.

It looked perfect!

For the first time in weeks, she felt happy.

After that, Hildegarde spent all her spare time designing clothes. During the daytime, she sewed identical Great Green Shirts. But she lived for the one-of-a-kind clothes she made at home.

Best of all, Mr. Arno's voice stopped echoing in her head.

She was able to sleep again!

This continued until the day Hildegarde ran out of clean green shirts to wear to work.

She wore one of her own creations and tried to look inconspicuous.

Luckily, Mr. Arno was away at the Hoof and Mouth Conference for two days!

Trying to finish her 250 shirts as fast as she could, Hildegarde felt a tap on her shoulder. It was Maybelle, who worked at the next sewing machine.

"Your sweater is beautiful!"

Hildegarde peered out from behind her stack of Great Green Shirts. Maybelle wasn't alone! All 138 of the other ewes had stopped their work to admire the sweater too.

"It's so wonderful to have a change from these boring green shirts!" cried Toola.

Hildegarde couldn't stop herself. She blurted, "I have other things too! Tomorrow at lunch, let's have a fashion show!"

"Fashion show!"

The fashion show was
a smashing success.

Every ewe wore
a different outfit.

Hildegarde
had designed
and made
them all.

Toola strutted by.

"I feel so special!"

Everyone said

"Ooooooh!"

Maybelle whirled at the end of the catwalk.

"I'm ME! I'm not just a NUMBER!"

Everyone said "Baaaaaaa!"

When Hildegarde came out, everyone cheered.

They sang songs...

and talked...
and ate lunch.

What fun
they were
having!

Hildegarde knew her clothes were as great
as Great Green Shirts. Or even greater!

She stood up straight. "I'm NOT a troublemaker.
And my clothes AREN'T TRASH."

Everything stopped,
including Mr. Arno.

The room behind him
fell deadly silent.

He glanced
around...

and gulped.

139 pairs of eyes glared back at him. None of them were friendly. Maybelle cleared her throat.

"You're just a bully. You couldn't even dream up clothes this beautiful, let alone create them!"

Toola chimed in.

"You prefer these plain green shirts, Mr. Arno.
But that's just your opinion. I would choose
Hildegarde's clothes any day!"

Everyone nodded.

Hildegarde smiled.

"Face it, Mr. Arno! Sheep like variety!"

She turned to the other ewes.

"I'm going to set up my own clothing business!
We'll make fantastic clothes in all sorts of colors and styles.
It looks like I have customers, but I'll need employees!"

"Let's go!"

All the ewes flocked to the exit.

Mr. Arno's head throbbed.

His eyes crossed
with confusion.

"Hildegarde, what makes
you think you can do this?

You're just a ewe."

Hildegarde looked around.

The ewes' new clothes sparkled in the afternoon sunshine.

"That's right," she replied.

"I'M ME!"